Paper Son

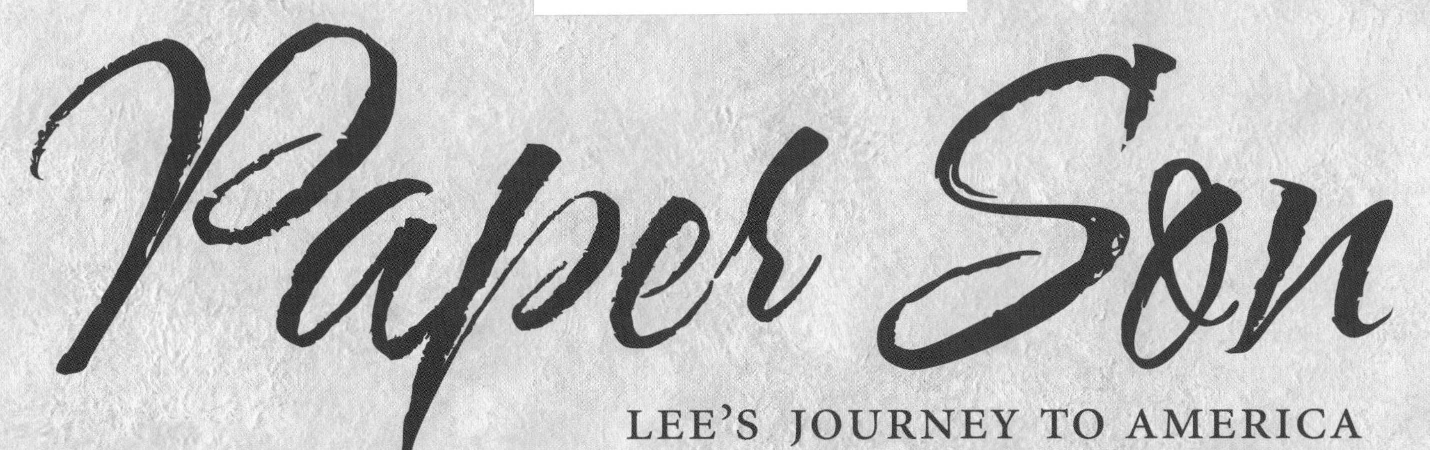

LEE'S JOURNEY TO AMERICA

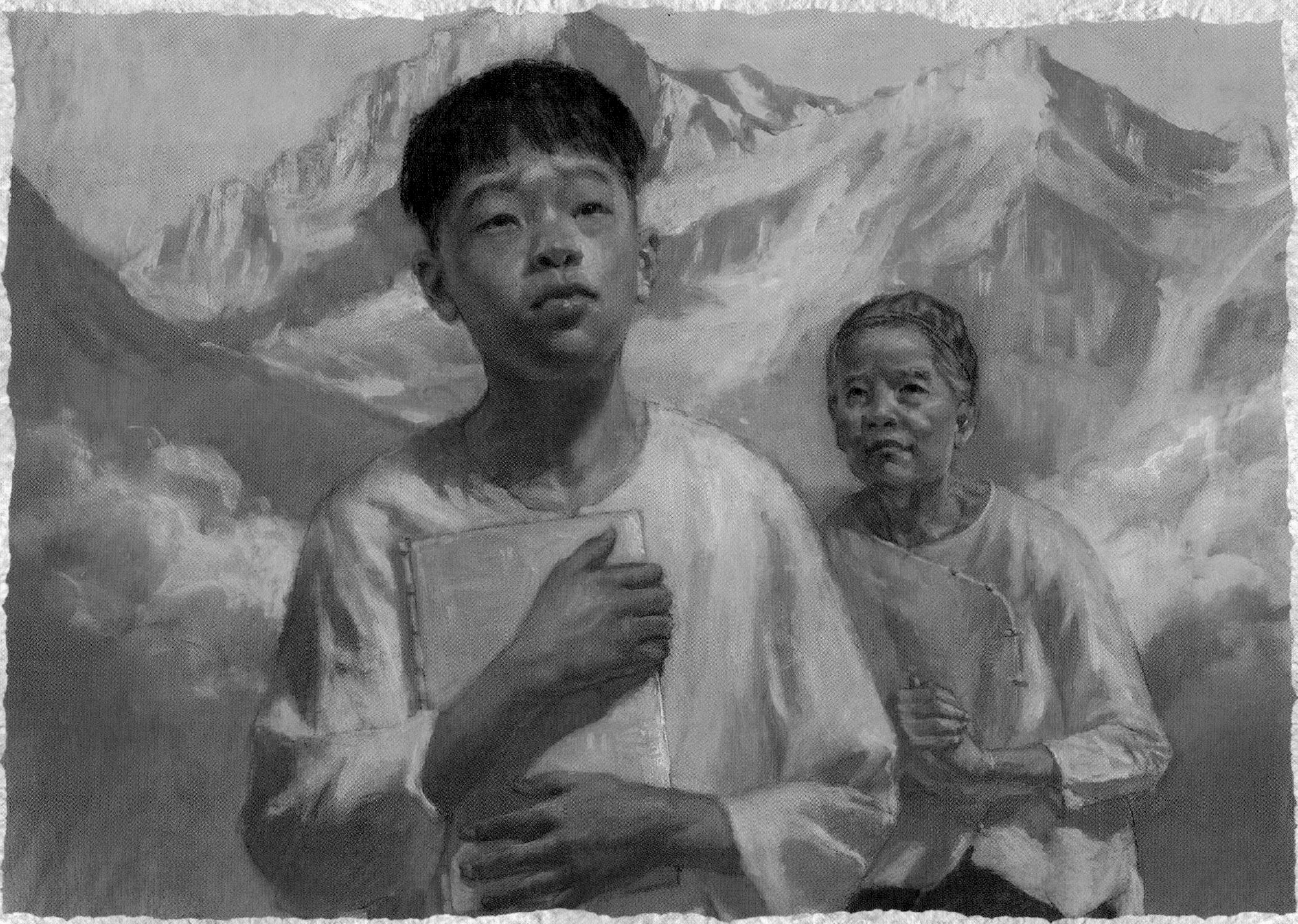

Written by Helen Foster James & Virginia Shin-Mui Loh
Illustrated by Wilson Ong

SLEEPING BEAR PRESS
TALES *of* YOUNG AMERICANS SERIES

For Larry Dane Brimner, Pam Muñoz Ryan, Jean Ferris, Kathleen Krull, Paul Brewer, and Deborah Halverson.
—Helen

To my husband, Jeffrey Hagan.
—Virginia

To my father, who dreamed of coming to America, so that his posterity could dream.
—Wilson

Sleeping Bear Press gratefully acknowledges and thanks Ying Manrique for her assistance in translating the Chinese characters that are depicted on the walls of the Angel Island dormitories.

The translation of the quote on page 20: "How was I to know I would become a prisoner suffering in the wooden building?" is from the book *Island: Poetry and History of Chinese Immigrants on Angel Island, 1910–1940* by Him Mark Lai, Genny Lim, and Judy Yung, published by University of Washington Press (Seattle and London).

Sleeping Bear Press
315 E. Eisenhower Parkway, Suite 200
Ann Arbor, MI 48108
www.sleepingbearpress.com

Printed and bound in the United States.

10 9 8 7 6 5 4 3 2 1

Library of Congress Cataloging-in-Publication Data

James, Helen Foster, 1951-
Paper son : Lee's journey to America / written by Helen Foster James and Virginia Shin-Mui Loh ; illustrated by Wilson Ong.
p. cm.
Summary: Twelve-year-old Lee, an orphan, reluctantly leaves his grandparents in China for the long sea voyage to San Francisco, where he and other immigrants undergo examinations at Angel Island Immigration Station.
ISBN 978-1-58536-833-4
[1. Emigration and immigration—Fiction. 2. Immigrants—Fiction. 3. Angel Island Immigration Station (Calif.)—Fiction 4. Chinese Americans—Fiction. 5. Orphans—Fiction. 6. Angel Island (Calif.)—History—20th century—Fiction.]
I. Loh, Virginia Shin-Mui. II. Ong, Wilson, ill. III. Title.
PZ7.J154115Pap 2013
[Fic]—dc23 2012033691

"What's this?" Lee thumbed through pages of Chinese words, telling another person's story.

"Your coaching book. You must learn every detail. You'll be questioned in *Gum Saan*." PoPo touched Lee's cheek. "You'll leave for America in three weeks."

"Why can't I stay here with you and Gong Gong?" Lee had just celebrated his twelfth birthday but felt little and lost at the thought of leaving his grandparents.

"Before your parents were killed by bandits, they bought you a paper son slot from Uncle Fu. They spent all their money and borrowed the rest. Gong Gong and I have been saving money to pay off their debts."

"How much did it cost?"

"One hundred dollars for each of your years."

"That's too much money! Can we get it back?" Lee knew they needed farm equipment and a new roof. He remembered nights he'd gone hungry dreaming of steamed fish with brown sauce and long noodles with chicken and bok choy.

"This is better for your future, our future. Look at the Chans. Chan Ho was sent to *Gum Saan.* Now he sends money home every month. They never worry about being hungry."

"I don't want to go!"

"In *Gum Saan*, mountains are topped with gold and streets are paved with silver. Our mountains are topped with wars and our streets are paved with bandits. Gong Gong and I are old and sick. This is no place for you."

"How will you work our land without me?"

"We'll manage. You must go and make us proud."

Lee didn't want to travel to the Land of the Flowery Flag, but knew PoPo was speaking the truth. "I'll go to *Gum Saan* and send money for food and medicine. I'll make you proud."

PoPo wiped away a tear. "You've made me proud already."

"My name is Fu Lee. My father, Fu Ming, is an American. I was born on . . ." Lee studied his coaching book. He was no longer Wang Lee. He was Fu Lee, his *chi ming*, his paper son name. He would have a new family. He'd have to forget about PoPo and Gong Gong.

PoPo stopped her stitching. "In your heart you'll always belong to me."

Lee memorized every detail about his paper family: The village temple faced southeast. Their clock sits to the right of the family portrait on the altar.

Every night PoPo quizzed Lee. "How many windows are in the Fu house?"

"Three."

"No, there are three doors and five windows. Study more," PoPo scolded. "*Gum Saan* men ask your paper father the same questions. They compare answers. You must convince them you're Fu's real son. Otherwise . . ."

". . . We'll lose the money and I'll be deported."

PoPo continued stitching. "No need to think about that. You'll make us proud."

Lee traveled to Canton where he boarded a train to Hong Kong. He marked the day in his mind: The Year of the Tiger, 1926, four days before the Lantern Festival.

In Hong Kong, Lee boarded a large ship called the *S.S. President Lincoln.* He would rather be on the farm, rubbing PoPo's feet and listening to Gong Gong's stories. His fingers traced the rim of his cap, feeling PoPo's careful stitching.

Lee spent his days on deck, away from the stale dampness of his quarters. He spent nights dreaming of his true family, but details of Fu's village filled his mind. "My name is Fu Lee. My father, Fu Ming, is an American. I was born on . . ."

On the twenty-first day, a booming voice shouted, "I see land! *Gum Saan!*"

Lee remembered PoPo's words: *Don't trust anyone. Don't let anyone see your coaching book.* If people saw it, they'd know he was a paper son. Lee dropped his coaching book into the chilly waters.

In San Francisco, Lee and other Chinese were taken on a small boat to the Angel Island Immigration Station. Lee's sea legs felt like limp bamboo as he walked on the dock.

Guards, *luk yi,* barked orders. An interpreter repeated them in Chinese. "Men to the right. Girls to the left."

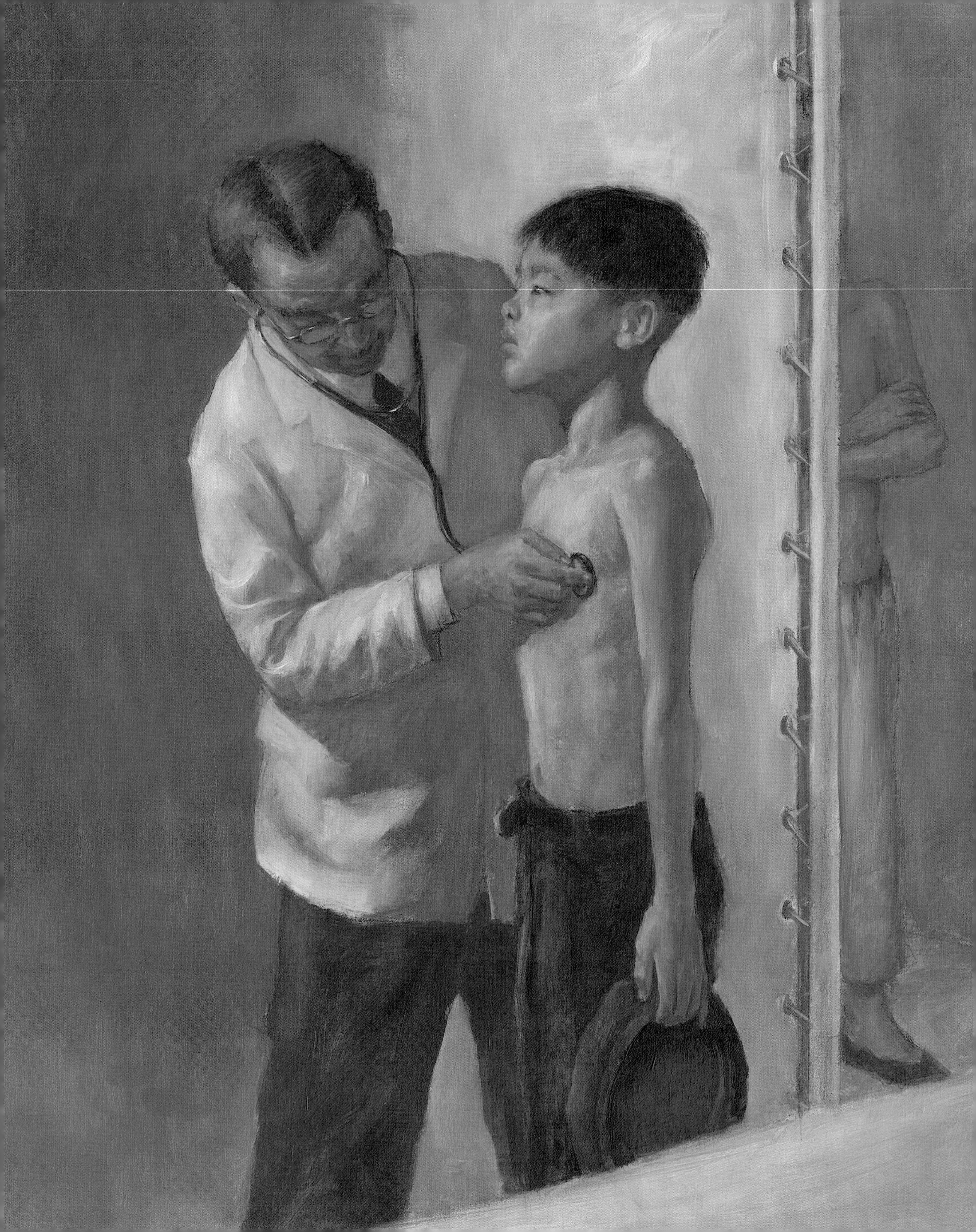

The men and boys formed a line for medical exams. They took off their shirts. Lee felt ashamed. A man put a cold, metal circle on his chest. He poked and prodded.

Lee noticed two men and a boy were sent to one side of the room. They were coughing. He heard whispering. "They'll be returned to China. Such shame." Lee stood tall and looked strong.

The examiner nodded at Lee and pointed to the side of the room with healthy people. Lee's heartbeat calmed.

More orders were barked. “Follow me to your dormitory.” They were led to the wood house, *muk uk*. Inside, metal beds were stacked three high. The lowest bunk was Lee’s.

Everywhere a hand could reach words were carved or written on the walls, telling stories of people who had been here before. Lee ran his hand over the Chinese characters, reading them aloud. *“Imprisoned in this wooden building, I am always sad and bored.”*

木屋拘留幾十天
從今遠別此樓

A head poked down from the bunk above and said in a familiar dialect, "Read more. Practice your reading."

"Who are you?"

"Call me Tai."

Lee read while Tai listened. "*It's a pity for heroes to be contained. We can only wait …*"

With a BANG, a guard placed a bar across the door.

In the morning, the guard removed the bar. Everyone walked in line to the dining hall. Hungry, Lee ate the tasteless *jook,* rice porridge.

In the yard Lee recalled each fact in his coaching book. He saw others sitting alone and wondered if they were doing the same.

An older boy grabbed Lee's cap. "Here, catch this!" he yelled to another boy.

Lee shouted, "Give it back. Give it back now!"

The boys laughed while Lee shuttled between them begging for his cap, his only reminder of PoPo and his real life.

Lee fought back tears trying to grab his cap.

Tai stepped between the boys, intercepting Lee's cap.

"Take better care of your belongings." Before Lee could thank him, Tai was gone.

Lee joined Tai on the bench and pointed to a newspaper. “Are you going to read that?”

“Practice. Read it to me.”

Lee read to Tai.

Tai asked, “Can I trust you?”

Lee remembered PoPo’s words: *Don’t trust anyone.*

But Tai had helped him with those two mean boys. Lee nodded.

Tai handed Lee an orange. Inside the orange peel was a note.

“Where did you get this?”

Tai said, “My *father* paid kitchen help to pass this to me. Can you read it?”

Lee nodded and read the tiny Chinese characters, “Baby niece born two months ago. Name is Mui.”

Tai bowed his head, repeating the words.

Lee whispered, “You’re a paper son.”

Tai’s face changed. “Don’t say that.”

“It’s okay,” Lee whispered. “So am I.”

“Be careful who you talk to. Don’t trust anyone.”

Weeks later, Lee was called into the interrogation room. His stomach churned. One small mistake and he would be sent back to China.

The interrogator asked questions. An interpreter repeated each question in Chinese.

"What's your name?"

"Fu Lee."

"What's your father's name?

"Fu Ming."

"Where was he born?"

"San Francisco. In Chinatown."

"How many windows are in your house?"

"Three. No, five."

The men looked at each other. Lee took a deep breath.

"Three? Five? What's your answer?"

"I'm sorry. I'm nervous. There are three doors. Five windows."

"Where is the rice bin?"

"On the right side of the kitchen door."

"Where do you sleep?"

"In the bedroom I share with my cousin."

They asked questions for hours. Lee grew tired and confused. His cap slipped from his nervous fingers. The interpreter picked it up.

He whispered, "Hide this. Don't bring it into this room again. Trust me."

Lee took his cap and nodded, confused as he remembered PoPo and Tai's words to not trust anyone.

The interrogators talked in hushed voices. Lee couldn't understand. He studied their faces.

Finally, the interpreter spoke, "You may return to the dormitory."

Questions consumed Lee's thoughts and tied up his stomach. *Did I answer the questions right? Did I say anything wrong?*

A week later, a guard led Lee to the interrogation room again.

The interrogator stared at Lee. “Your father said the rice bin was to the left of the door, not the right.”

“We moved it since he left China. Rain damaged the left side of the door. My father wouldn’t have known that,” Lee answered confidently, even though he wasn’t.

The interrogator asked one last question. “Why do you want to live here?”

Lee was nervous. This wasn’t one of the answers he’d studied. He decided to tell the truth.

“I want to make my family proud. There are more opportunities in America.”

Three days later the guard opened the dormitory's door and called, "Fu Lee."

The interpreter was waiting for him. "The interrogators liked your last answer. Good fortune to you in *Gum Saan*." Then he whispered, "You remind me of my own little boy."

Lee bowed to him and returned to the dormitory.

本木
打算
来

"Are you going to be landed?" Tai asked.

"Yes. Tomorrow."

"Why are you sad? People have been waiting months to leave this place."

Lee wanted to tell Tai how a part of him wished he'd failed questions so he could return to China, to PoPo and Gong Gong. "I'm scared. I've never met my *father*."

"Trust me. You'll be fine." Tai smiled. "I didn't want to come either, but now I need to stay."

That night Lee added their story to the wall: *"I didn't want to come, but now I need to stay."*

In the morning Lee gathered his belongings. He felt his cap's rim and read PoPo's tiny secret stitching: "Trust your heart."

Lee put on his cap and walked out of the wood house. He was landed.

In San Francisco his new future greeted him. Lee welcomed his paper father like PoPo had taught him. "Hello. My name is Fu Lee. My father, Fu Ming, is an American and so am I."

Angel Island History

Angel Island is sometimes referred to as the "Ellis Island of the West"; however, the immigrant experience was quite different. Angel Island was the first stop for immigrants who entered America crossing the Pacific Ocean. They were processed through Angel Island Immigration Station between 1910 and 1940 when it was closed.

Chinese came to *Gum Saan*, Gold Mountain (the name they gave to California), to seek fortunes and escape misfortunes. They were not welcomed. In 1882 the United States Congress enacted the Chinese Exclusion Act to prevent Chinese from immigrating.

China was besieged by droughts, floods, famine, economic disasters, political turmoil, bandits, and wars. Homes and livelihoods were destroyed. For many, coming to America was their only option.

San Francisco's earthquake and fire in 1906 destroyed many official birth records. Some Chinese living in America created paper immigration "slots" to help immigrants claim citizenship. This allowed Chinese children to come to America as a "paper son" or, less frequently, "paper daughter." Their families bought papers from U.S. residents stating they were related, but the relationship was only on paper.

The papers (or coaching book) detailed information about their "family." On Angel Island, immigrants were interrogated for hours about their family. If they couldn't answer the questions, they were deported. Sometimes Chinese kitchen workers helped immigrants by sneaking possible questions and answers to detainees under a bowl of soup or on a tiny note tucked within an orange peel. Chinese immigrants were detained here for weeks or months. Some of these detainees carved poems on the walls telling their experiences.

Angel Island Immigration Station is now a National Historic Landmark. For more information about this fascinating place and time in history, visit the Angel Island Immigration Station Foundation's website at www.aiisf.org.